Randy the Raindrop by Patty Jean Wiese

Copyright © 2012 Patty Jean Wiese

ISBN: 1-45-635101-X
ISBN13: 978-1-456351-0-14
Library of Congress Control Number: 2010917151
CreateSpace Independent Publishing Platform
North Charleston, South Carolina

10 9 8 7 6 5 4 3 2 1

Published by Stormy Day Books
www.StormyDayBooks.com
Illustrated by Kim Sponaugle
Edited by Jill Ronsley, suneditwrite.com
Printed by CreateSpace, North Charleston, SC

Printed and bound in the USA

Randy the Raindrop

I'm a little raindrop!

Written by Patty Jean Wiese
Illustrated by Kim Sponaugle

This book is dedicated to all the children in the world.

I'll see you soon, my rainy day friend,
And think of you when the raindrops end.
I'll have a raindrop day with you.
You're my special friend—it's oh so true!
This story's just for you.

Sometimes I'm BIG, sometimes I'm small,
Sometimes you barely see me at all.
Big or small, tiny or tall—
It all depends on the way I fall.

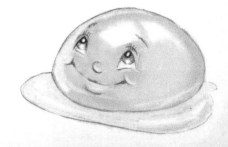

I'm a little raindrop
falling to the ground.
I don't know where I'm going
or whether I'll be found.

I might drop down
from the clouds
one day

Into your backyard,
where you laugh
and play.

Billy brought his baseball and bat to the park.

Buster ran along with him to jump and bark.

For you and your friends there will be no rain today.

So you can have a game—let's all go play!

Judy jumped a puddle in the park nearby.
Gosh! What a splash! They're soaked! Oh my!
They laughed so hard 'cause they didn't feel wet.
Their raincoats kept them dry, I bet.

I'm a little raindrop
falling all around.

I'm here, there
and everywhere,
and finally
on the ground.

When you look straight up to the big bright sky,
Give me a wave, and please say "Hi!"

Suzy saw me dropping, dropping to the ground.

She caught me with her raincoat, dancing all around.

I landed on her shoulder with a splash and a smile.

Would you like to play with me for a while?

Robby rode his bicycle
early one night.
I landed on the handle bars
and held on very tight.
As fast as lightning! Whee ...!
Here we go!
Riding all around and
everywhere we know.

Up and down we bounced—I felt that we could fly
Until Robby stopped—then we laughed
and said, "Goodbye."
It all was so much fun.
We really had a blast
Playing in the wind
and riding so fast.

I sometimes go to China,
or all the way to Spain.

But I always come back home
so that you can hear the rain.
Then from L.A. I sail to Bombay
I can do all that in just one day.
Hooray!

If the clouds go away
and it's sunny all day,
I turn itty-bitty
floating up and away.
That's the main reason
why I love to fly high,
Up towards the sun
and the big blue sky.

When the clouds are raining and you *see* me fall
Outside your window, just give me a call.
We'll have a lot of fun before I have to go,
When the sun comes out to say "Hello."

First day, second day,
raining on and on.
Third day, fourth day,
rain will soon be gone.

I'll be back another day
to play a game with you.
We'll have a raindrop day
full of fun for two!

I'm a Little Raindrop

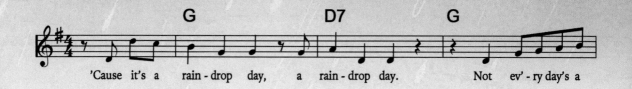

'Cause it's a rain-drop day, a rain-drop day. Not ev'-ry day's a

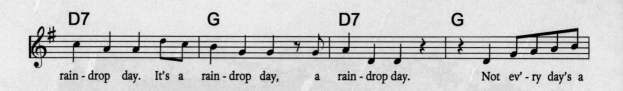

rain-drop day. It's a rain-drop day, a rain-drop day. Not ev'-ry day's a

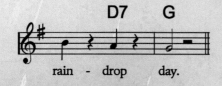

rain - drop day.

Visit Randy's website to listen to the song

"I'm a Little Raindrop"

and download a free copy

of the music sheet!

www.RandytheRaindrop.com

Randy's Weather Facts

What is rain?

Water always exists in the air, but it's too tiny for us to see. This is called water vapor. When the vapor cools, it turns into clouds and falls to the earth as rain.

Where does the most rain fall each year?

On Mount Waialeale, a mountain on an Island called Kauai in the middle of the Hawaiian Islands. Every year, it rains an average of 450 to 512 inches, or 40 feet. Rain falls from 335 to 360 days each year. Because a year has 365 days, it rains almost every day. Kauai's nickname is "Garden Island" because all the rain makes the island very green and rich.

What are clouds?

A cloud is a large collection of tiny droplets of water attached to tiny dust particles in the air called nuclei. When it's cold enough, they become ice crystals. The droplets are so small and light that they float in the air.

What is a rainbow?

Sunlight is made of all the colors visible to the eye. When the whole range of sunlight colors are combined, the light looks white to us. "Refracted sunlight" is white light split into all its color groups. A rainbow has colors because it is sunlight refracted off of tiny water droplets.

A rainbow is said to have seven colors—red, orange, yellow, green, blue, indigo and violet. Actually, a rainbow has thousands of colors from red to violet and even more colors than the eye can see. This was first explained and demonstrated by Sir Isaac Newton in 1666.

Where is the sun when you see a rainbow?

The sun is always behind you when you face a rainbow. The rain is in the direction of the rainbow.

For more of Randy's Weather Facts and Fun, visit his website: www.RandytheRaindrop.com

Find out how much it rains where you live and say hi to Randy the Raindrop.

Patty Jean Wiese has loved to write since she was a child. Her meteorologist husband's "weather on the brain" has rubbed off on her and inspired her fun weather characters for children. Patty, who enjoys caring for animals, loves the outdoors and gardening, and resides in Portland, Oregon, with their dog Buster.

Kim Sponaugle is known for her bright, playful illustrations and lovable character expressions that celebrate the joys of childhood. She has illustrated more than thirty books for kids including, *The Adventures of Beatrice series, Gazillions Bunches, Oodles & Tons* and Global eBook award winner *Angel Eyes*, but *Randy the Raindrop—I'm a Little Raindrop* is one of her favorites. Kim resides with her family in Salem County, New Jersey.

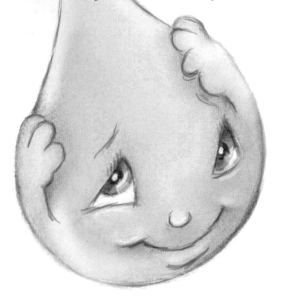

"He covers the heavens with clouds; he prepares rain for the earth; He makes grass grow on the hills."

—Psalm 147:8

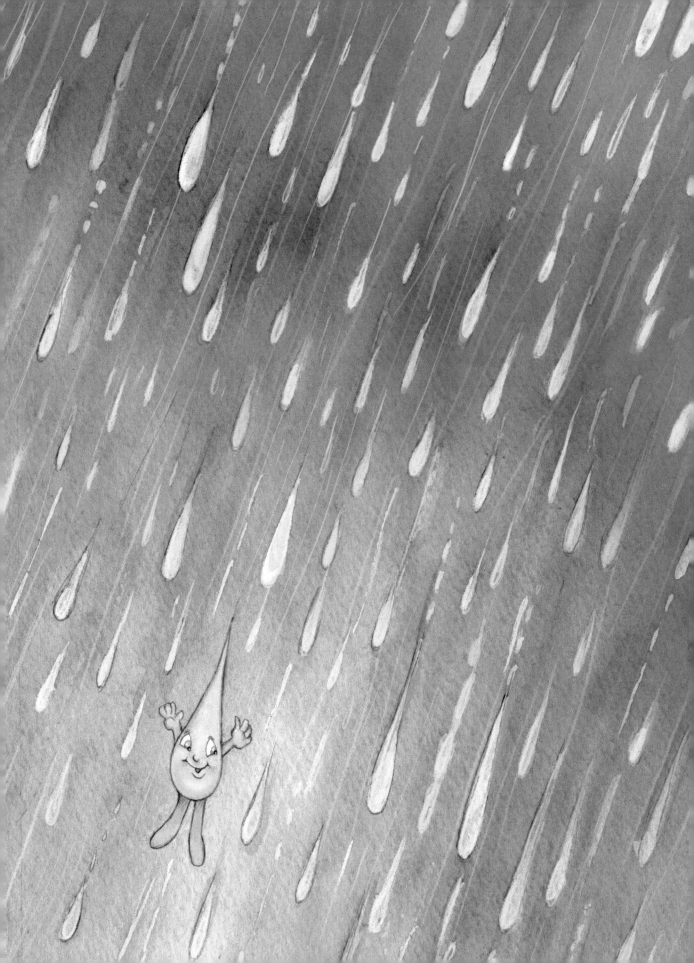

Made in the USA
Columbia, SC
11 October 2020